THE QUEST

BOOK ONE IN THE ANGEL CHRONICLES SERIES

ESTER LÓPEZ

Writing & Photographic Services LLC

Published by Writing & Photographic Services, LLC

Cover Design Copyright 2019 by ebooklaunch.com
ISBN: 978-0-9970033-8-3

THE QUEST

is a re-telling of the story of
TOBIT

*This book is lovingly dedicated to all those who believe in Angels
and the power of prayer.*

ABOUT THE AUTHOR

To keep up to date on the author's book releases and book signings, please join Ester's Readers Group at:
www.esterlopez.com

Follow Ester's Blogs at:
www.esterlopez.com
www.authorblogspot.esterlopez.com

Follow Ester on:
Twitter: @esterlopez1
Facebook: EsterLopezAuthor

And if you like the story, please give an honest review at your favorite retailer.

1

———

"I'm really sorry guys." Toby apologized.

"Football is not your game, Toby," Mike said, patting him on the back.

He nodded. He knew it was true, that's why he never tried out for the team. But just hanging out with the guys helped soften the stress of studying.

"It's okay," Lucas said, patting him on the back like Mike had. "It's just a game."

"Some people take it seriously," Toby said. He glanced up at the blue sky and let the sun's rays penetrate his skin. Closing his eyes, he inhaled the spring air and tried to let these memories burn into his mind. Graduation would be bittersweet.

"Are your parents coming for graduation?" Lucas asked, bringing him out of his thoughts.

Reality set in. "Since my dad's accident, my parents don't travel anymore, except to the doctor."

"Sorry to hear that," Lucas said. "My family will be here and I want you to meet them."

"Sure, I'd like that." Toby meant it. Lucas was not only a

dorm-mate but his roommate. They got along great even though they majored in different areas. He would miss having him around.

Toby glanced at his surroundings, taking in the last visions of his dorm and the nearby buildings. Middle Tennessee State University had been his home for the past four years. He looked forward to the next stage in his life.

Now, it was imperative he find a job so he could help support his parents. What he didn't tell Lucas was his dad used to be a professor at this very university, before the accident.

But that accident changed everything for his father. An organized man who planned well for every contingency was now in chaos. He relied on his wife to keep him in some type of order, but Toby knew his father needed more than that to feel normal.

He and Lucas headed back to their dorm.

Once inside, Toby began packing up his memories and his life. He separated things he couldn't part with, first. Then, he concentrated on things he could live without. By night-fall, he had re-packed his Volkswagen bug at least four times.

The next day, Toby finished packing the last box into his car and headed back to his dorm to get ready for the cere-monies. Lucas was still packing some clothes into a box when Toby entered the room. A man stood beside Lucas.

"Dad, this is my roommate, Toby Flint."

Toby reached out his hand. "Nice to meet you, sir," he said.

Mr. Cane shook Toby's hand. "Lucas speaks highly of you," he said.

Toby cut a glance at Lucas and Lucas shrugged.

"Well, I better go so I can find our seats. Your mother and siblings are all waiting for me at the hall."

"Sure, Dad."

Toby and Lucas put on their ceremonial garb and headed to the auditorium. Excitement and anxiety hit Toby all at once.

"So, are you headed home after this?" Lucas asked.

"Yes. I was hoping I would hear something from at least one of the elementary schools I applied to teach at before I left, but no one has called."

"I'm heading home, too. I've got some prospects back home that I've heard from, so I'll see what happens."

"Good luck, Lucas, and don't lose my number. I expect to hear from you as soon as you land a job."

"You, too, buddy." Lucas gave Toby a hug before they separated to go on stage.

After a lengthy, speech-filled period, the graduates were finally called to receive their degrees. This ceremony couldn't end fast enough for him. Toby noticed all the parents who were in the audience waiting for their son or daughter to get their degree. He felt a little sadness that his parents couldn't be here for this special day in his life, but he thought of his high school graduation and that would have to sustain him. He knew they were proud of him. He just felt cheated of sharing this moment with his parents.

Afterward, Toby ran into Lucas and his family. They got a few pictures together with their phones before they separated.

Toby headed back to his dorm after dropping off his cap and gown. If it hadn't been for his father's accident, both his parents would be here and he would be celebrating with them.

Toby's phone rang, bringing him out of his slump.

"Hello?"

"Is this Toby Flint?"

"Yes, it is. How can I help you?"

"Toby, this is Gerald Haynes. We met at the career fair this past fall."

"Yes, sir. I remember you." He had been hoping for this call.

"We'd like to set up an appointment with you to talk further about teaching at our campus."

"I'd like that." Toby tried to remain calm, despite the urge to jump up and down with excitement.

"Let's say, next Thursday at 1pm?"

"That sounds perfect. Where do you want to meet?"

"Well, we're in Arizona. I'll text you my address and phone number."

Toby was elated with the news, but where would he get the money to travel to Arizona and pay for a hotel room?

After arriving back at his dorm, Toby gave his room the once over to make sure he wasn't leaving anything behind and headed for his car. The sadness of leaving was now overwhelmed by the excitement of this new opportunity. Would he earn enough to survive on his own and take care of both his parents? Would he have to move his parents to Arizona?

A new set of thoughts came to mind. He would have to find a place to live. And moving himself to Arizona was half done since everything he owned was now in this car.

The drive home took a little over an hour. He couldn't believe his father had driven this route twice a day, every day, for all the years he taught, but it was relaxing.

Tennessee had lots of trees and hills and the view of the countryside was always beautiful. The different hues of green new leaves announced spring in all its glory.

His phone rang. When Toby saw who was calling, he pulled over to the side of the road.

2

———

Tobias Flint sat in his favorite chair, staring straight ahead, as his wife, Anna, read the letter.

"We have until next week to pay the mortgage or they foreclose on the house," she said.

Tobias ran his hand through his graying hair. He desperately needed a shave. "And the savings?"

"We closed the account months ago because there was no money. Remember?"

"What about your Social Security?"

"I'm not old enough, I told you that."

"My disability?" He grabbed the arms of the chair and squeezed.

"We're still waiting to hear from them. It's a process and it takes a while."

"Call them again, we don't have time to wait on them, Anna." He squeezed the arms harder.

"What about your college friend, Anthony Zacarias?"

"Anthony?" His grip on the arms lessened. "Yes! I forgot all about him. I have to find his number. Where's my phone, Anna. I must call him."

Tobias had known Anthony since college. The memory of his first summer job came to mind. He trusted Anthony with some money to invest and when Anthony's investment paid off, he had earned more from the investment than working all summer in a restaurant making good tips. He told Anthony to re-invest the earnings. Over the years, Anthony had kept him informed of the progress.

Anna Flint searched through the small Rolodex by the phone several times, trying different names. "Nothing in here. Try your phone."

Tobias opened a drawer beside his chair and pulled out his cell phone. He used its text to speech engine to search his contacts for Anthony, Tony, and Zacarias, with no luck.

"Did he have a nickname?" Anna asked.

"Tony," Tobias said, leaning forward in his seat. He hated this feeling of helplessness. He wanted his life the way it was but the blindness held him back.

"Have you tried that?" She asked.

"Yes, I tried that. They assured me they transferred everything when I changed phones."

"Well, they lied. Do you remember his area code? Maybe that will bring up his name."

"No. He moved from southern California to the middle somewhere."

Anna searched for Anthony Zacarias on her phone under the Google App with no luck. "What about your scrapbook? Would his number be in there?

"Try it, Anna. And look through our yearbook as well."

Anna searched under both books with no luck.

"I'm going to go through your files and see what I come up with," she said.

• • •

It was over an hour before Anna gave up her search. She sat next to Tobias in her own chair. "Tell me what you remember about Anthony," she said. She gently covered his hand with hers.

"We were roommates. He was a sloppy mess but good with numbers. Both of us worked in town during the summer break."

"What did you do?" Anna asked.

"I worked in a small restaurant while Anthony worked with an accounting firm."

Anna saw Tobias' face light up as he talked about his friend.

"Anthony had hunches about investing and talked me into joining him in a venture. We both put in a week's pay. By the end of the summer, we made more money from our investment than we did from working all summer."

"What did you do with your money?"

"I gave it to Anthony and told him to re-invest it. I hadn't thought much about it since then."

"Since you were in college?" Anna asked.

"Well, whenever I called him, he updated me on the progress. It's been awhile since I called him, though."

"Do you know what town he lives in?" Anna asked.

"No. The last time we talked...all I remember is he still lives in California."

"Let's put this in the Lord's hands, Tobias," she said. "My small paychecks allow us to eat and pay the electric bill, but it's not enough for the mortgage payment, let alone the three months in arrears." Anna reached for Tobias' hand and closed her eyes in prayer.

Tobias began, "Lord, you know our situation and my condition. We put all of this in your hands and beg you to take pity on me and Anna, your humble servants, in Jesus' name we pray."

"Amen."

3

————

Toby answered his phone. "Hi Dad! Is everything all right?"

"Health wise, everything is the same."

"Otherwise?"

"We just got a letter from the bank, son, and things are not so good."

"What's happened?"

"The bank will foreclose on our house in one week unless we pay the mortgage."

"Why haven't you paid it, Dad?"

"I'm no longer getting Workers' Comp and my disability hasn't kicked in yet."

"How long has this been going on?"

"Three months."

"Why didn't you tell me before now?

"I didn't want to worry you since you had exams."

"I could have found a job, Dad. I could have helped you."

"Your school is more important."

"More important than living on the streets?"

"When is the graduation ceremony?"

"It was this morning, Dad."

"Why didn't you tell us?"

"Would you have come?"

"You know I'm blind and your mother doesn't drive long distances."

"That's why I didn't tell you."

"I'm sorry I missed it, Toby. It was your big day and I should've been there for you."

Toby squeezed the tears from his eyes. His heart swelled.

"I'm really proud of you and your accomplishments, son."

"Thanks, Dad." He choked out the words.

"I really need you to come home. I may have an idea of how to get a hold of some money."

"I'm heading there now, Dad. I should be home shortly."

His good news about the teaching job could wait. Somehow, this day wasn't turning out the way he envisioned it.

4

———

ara Duggan lived with her parents above their diner and gas station just outside Las Cruces, New Mexico. The diner sat back off the road but faced it. Their apartment faced the mountains in the other direction, with a hundred-foot drop-off out back.

One of the few employees who had been with the family for years made a comment to a customer when she didn't realize that Sara was in the diner, listening.

"Yes," she whispered. "The rumors are true. Sara has been married three times. If you ask me, I think she's cursed."

"Why do you say that?" the customer whispered back.

"Because each bridegroom threw himself out the window to his death before consummating the marriage."

"Three times?"

"Yes. Either that or she threw them out the window herself."

"She doesn't look strong enough to do something like that," the customer argued.

"Well, better for us that she never bears children. She's quite homely."

Sara entered the diner from the back of the kitchen. Karen's words still burned her ears. She swallowed hard and set the stack of dishes down on the counter and quickly ran outside the diner, heading for the gas station bathroom.

Why did her parents keep Karen working there? She had been hateful to her since she was a child. Sara locked herself in the bathroom. She stood on the toilet seat and threw her apron over the rafter, wrapping the loose end around her neck.

The thought occurred to her that her parents would be blamed if she ended her own life. She loosened the apron and sat upon the toilet seat and prayed.

"Lord, help me! Take my life this night or take pity on me."

If she had a car, she would drive off and never come back. She certainly couldn't go inside to face Karen and the customers, not after what she heard.

"Sara?" her mother called from outside the bathroom.

"In a minute," she called out, wiping the tears from her face. She quickly unlocked the door, her apron slung over her shoulder.

"Mom, I'm not feeling well," she began.

"I heard," Miriam said. "Go on upstairs and rest. Your father and I will discuss this tonight." Miriam gave Sara a big hug, then watched as Sara slipped inside the apartment's front door.

5

———

Toby arrived home and his parents greeted him. He debated on unloading his things from the car when his mother called out to him.

"Toby, come inside. We have something to talk to you about."

While his mother went into the kitchen, Toby sat beside his father, in his mother's favorite chair.

"What is it, Dad? What did you and Mom want to talk to me about?" His mother came in with some iced tea and handed one to him and his father.

"Thanks, Mom."

Tobias cleared his throat. "Always strive to be an honorable man, Toby," his father began.

"Yes, sir."

"And I want you to give us both an honorable funeral."

"What? Are you two dying of something?"

"No, I meant when the time comes. Always be faithful to God."

"I am, or I try to be."

"Never entertain sin or transgression."

"Dad!"

"Always do good works and set aside money for charity."

"Is this a goodbye speech?"

"No. It's a father/son conversation about becoming a man."

"Dad, I think we should have had this conversation years ago, before I started college." Toby leaned forward in his seat. "You've always set good examples for me. I think I can do this."

Tobias raked his hand through his hair. "You're right. Well, at least I tried to set a good example."

Anna leaned forward in her seat. "Tell him your idea, Tobias."

"Yes, your mother is right. I had a dear friend in college who was good at investing money. I gave him my summer earnings from his first investment and told him to invest it all. I had completely forgotten about it until recently. If he was successful, I should have enough to pay my mortgage up to date and save the house."

"What about after that?" Toby asked.

"I should have my disability by then."

Anna looked down at her hands, folded in her lap. "I'm making enough to feed us and pay a bill, Toby." She glanced at Tobias. "I didn't tell your father, but I accepted the position of manager. I'll be making more money but I'll also be working more hours."

Tobias reached out to her and she grabbed his hand. "You'll have to learn to fend for yourself, Tobias."

He nodded.

"Who is this friend of yours?" Toby asked. Could this friend really help his father? Did he follow through and re-invest the money?

"His name is Anthony Zacarias. The last time we spoke, he lived in California."

"Do you have his number? I could call him for you?"

"No. I've lost his number, but your mother found a paper we both signed and tore in half. When you present this paper to him, he will know to pay you my investment."

"But California is a big state. Where would I start the search?"

"You have a phone and his name. He started an investment company years ago. Start there and maybe you can locate him."

"You're asking me to do something impossible, like finding a needle in a haystack. I wish you wouldn't pin all your hopes on him, dad."

"Oh, I'm not. God and you, son, are our only hope."

6

The next day, Toby headed out in his Volkswagen bug. His heart was heavy with the burden his father put on him. He didn't say it out loud, but he thought this idea was a waste of time.

He would stop in Arizona first for the job interview with Mr. Haynes on Thursday, then drive to California. His father didn't know he would be doing this, but it was on the way. Sort of. Why did this have to happen now?

He had a better chance of getting a teaching job in Arizona than his father had in this quest for his fortune in California. With all his father's talk about his friend, Anthony Zacarias, he forgot to tell him the good news about the job interview.

Last night, after he had emptied his car of all his belongings into his old room, he had re-packed for a week's trip. His plan was to sleep in his car at rest stops to save money for gas. He hated taking his mother's food money, but she insisted. She had packed him some healthy snacks and plenty of water as well. They put a lot of faith in this quest.

As he formed a plan in his mind, his car sputtered and slowed down, so he pulled off the road as it came to a stop.

He turned it off then tried to re-start it. It made an effort to start but didn't turn over. He tried again. This time, there was no sound.

"Great! Now what?" Toby got out of the car and lifted the hood. He glanced around for any stray wires. Everything looked good, but he had no idea how to fix a car. Especially, a VW.

A car whizzed by and he could feel the wind blow his hair and shake the small car. He walked around to his car door and heard a large truck braking. He looked up and saw a semi slowing down, pulling off the road. Instead of stopping behind his car, the truck stopped in front of it.

There was a small symbol on the door and the word 'Messenger' written across the back part of the truck.

Toby went to the trunk to search for any tool he might have, to bang on the battery cables, when a tall, dark-haired, tanned man walked up to him. He appeared to be Italian or European.

"Having problems?"

"It just stopped."

"Can I take a look at it?"

"Sure." Toby closed the trunk. "I don't even have any tools."

The slightly muscular man looked over the engine, wiggling hoses and touching wires. "Try starting it," he said.

Toby obliged and turned the key. Again, no sound but clicking.

"Hmmm. It could be your alternator." He pulled a crescent wrench out of his back pocket, tapping the battery cables, then the alternator. "Try it again."

Click, click, click.

"Whoa! How far are you going?"

"I was heading to Arizona and then California," Toby said.

"I've got to be in California in a few days to pick up a load. I can take you that far and maybe we can get someone to look at it there."

"That would be great but how do I get my car there?"

"Simple." The man walked over to the back of the truck, unlocking the doors. He lowered a ramp in front of the car.

"Put it in neutral."

Toby did what he said.

"You steer and push, I'll push," the man offered. He walked behind the VW bug and pushed.

Toby pushed as he steered the car up the ramp. It seemed much easier than he imagined. The car should be heavier, but it went up easily and smoothly. Toby put the car in Park and set the brake.

"Wow! Thanks! I don't know how to repay you."

"Don't worry about it. I could use the company." He wiped his hand on his jeans and then offered it to Toby. "I'm Raphael."

"Nice to meet you. I'm Toby."

"Hop in," Raphael gestured to his passenger side.

Toby pulled the door open and climbed in. The truck was clean inside, something he didn't expect of a truck driver, but the truck smelled new.

"Welcome aboard!" Raphael said to Toby, putting the truck in gear, he moved back onto the road.

"So, where are you from?" Raphael asked him.

"I'm from middle Tennessee," Toby said. "I just graduated college and I'm headed to an interview in Arizona."

"What was your major?"

"Education. I'm hoping to get a job in the Arizona school system. Then I can help my parents financially instead of..." Toby shook his head.

"Instead of what?"

"Instead of going on this quest for my father."

"Tell me about your father," Raphael said.

"He's a great guy, really. He used to be a professor at the university I attended. He had a car accident a few years ago which left him limping a little but blind."

"Sorry to hear that."

"Yeah, he used to be so organized. He planned well for his lessons, his days off, his vacation, but now, he seems to be in chaos because he can't see. He's been having a hard time dealing with the blindness."

"That would be hard for anyone."

"He walks with a cane and my mother doted on him initially, but she went back to work to help with the bills and he just can't deal with the blindness by himself. I think he expected my mother to be his eyes."

"So, what is this quest he's got you on?"

"He invested some money with a college friend years ago and wanted me to look him up. My dad lost his phone number and can only tell me his name. He's hoping that the investment panned out because he's about to lose his home if he doesn't come up with the money for the mortgage payment by next week."

"So, what's his friend's name?"

Toby pulled his phone out and did a search of his notes. "Anthony Zacarias."

"Tony? I know him. I can help you find him once we get there."

Toby turned in his seat and stared at Raphael. "This is amazing!" What luck to find just what he needed. "This is really hard to believe."

"Why is that?"

"I mean, to find you, someone who knows the very man I'm seeking, by accident."

"I find that when God has plans for you, He will put the right people in your path."

"Does that happen to you a lot?" Toby asked.

"All the time." Raphael turned and smiled. "Tell me more about your father."

Toby realized how keyed up he was about the quest and took a deep breath, letting it out slowly. "I really didn't want to go on this quest. I felt...put out by it, you know? I mean, I had plans, an interview. I could help my parents better that way than pinning their hopes on something that isn't a sure thing, you know?"

"It sounds more like your father had faith in his friend's ability, trusting God for the money he needed," Raphael said.

"The truth is, my dad is a great guy. He was always willing to help someone in need." Toby remembered some things from his past and felt more comfortable in sharing. "He used to take me with him on trips when he had to do research. I remember one time, when I was ten, there was a blind man on the street, begging for money. My father took him into a restaurant, bought him some dinner and asked the man how he could help make his life a little better. The man started to cry and told us his story. My father then took him to a church and spoke to the priest and they took him in."

"Your father is a caring person," Raphael said.

"Yes. I recall another time when we headed west and stopped at a diner in the middle of nowhere. This little girl spoke to me and showed me her drawings. They were amazing. I think we were both eight years old. We talked a long time while my father spoke to her parents. I felt a connection to her. She even gave me this necklace." He pulled it out from under his t-shirt. It was a half-heart with the word 'forever'. "Hers says, 'friends'."

"Impressive."

"It definitely made an impression on me. I still think about her and wonder what she's up to."

"Did you keep in touch?"

"No. I was just a kid. I didn't know how to write letters at the time. I don't even know where that place was."

Toby realized his feelings about the quest had softened. He really owed his dad big time for all the things he had done for him. All the things he learned and experienced.

Raphael yawned. "I think we'll camp here for the night." He pulled the rig over to a rest stop in a remote area. "There's a pond not far away and we can camp near it."

Raphael grabbed some equipment and a tent. He handed two sleeping bags to Toby. After a pit stop, the two headed to the pond area and pitched the tent. Toby tossed the two sleeping bags inside while Raphael rigged up a fishing pole.

"Make yourself useful and set this up." Raphael handed Toby a case containing a small propane stove, some pans, a small fold-up table, and some cooking supplies. By the time Toby had everything set up, Raphael walked up with several fish.

"That was fast."

Raphael cleaned the fish and handed some of the guts to Toby. "Put this in a plastic bag," he said.

"What is it?"

"It's the gall, heart, and liver of the fish. We'll need it later. They have curative properties."

"What could we possibly need this for?"

"You burn the fish's heart and liver and their smoke is used in the case of a man or woman plagued by a demon or evil spirit. Any such affliction disappears for good, leaving no trace."

"And the gall?"

"It's used as an eye ointment. After using it, you only have to blow on the white spots to cure them."

Toby did as Raphael said, placing the items into a baggy and setting it in the small cooler.

They feasted on fried fish and a couple of drinks. Toby cleaned up the mess and then crawled into the tent to sleep. Raphael was nowhere to be found.

7

———

Hours later, Toby awoke to Raphael's voice.

"Rise and shine!"

Toby sat up and noticed Raphael was not in the tent and neither was his sleeping bag. Daylight was just creeping over the horizon.

After rolling up his sleeping bag, he took the tent down and found Raphael waiting by the truck.

"Did you sleep well?" Raphael asked.

"Yes. I did. How about you?"

"Like I was sleeping on a cloud." Raphael climbed into the driver's side while Toby climbed into the passenger side.

Raphael drove until late afternoon, finally arriving at a small restaurant and gas station, somewhere in New Mexico.

Inside, there was an older man cooking, and an older woman behind the counter. A young woman was wiping down the tables.

The first thing Toby noticed were the large murals all over the walls. They depicted a story of some sort, with angels and demons fighting.

"Wow," Toby said aloud. "This artwork is amazing."

"Thank you," the young woman said. "Have a seat." She gestured to a nearby table in an otherwise empty restaurant.

"Who painted all these murals?" Toby asked.

"I did. Do you like them?"

"I love them. The work is incredible. Do you sell copies of your work?"

"No. I never thought of doing that."

"You should. I would love to own a copy of some of your work."

"Really?" She beamed. "My name is Sara and I'll be your server." She handed each of them a menu.

"Do you have a portfolio?" Raphael asked.

"Yes. I have smaller originals of all these. While you're deciding on your meal, I'll run and get it."

Toby glanced at Raphael.

"She lives here with her family," Raphael whispered.

"Have you been here before?

"Yes, many times."

"Raphael?" The cook called out, coming from behind the counter.

"Hello, Raj. This is Toby. Toby, Raj."

"Nice to meet you, sir." Toby stood and offered his hand to Raj.

"So, you like my daughter's work?"

"Yes, sir. It's beautiful. Inspiring."

"She gets bored in the slow months so we let her paint. It makes her happy."

"Okay, Dad. Don't spoil it," Sara said, returning with something in her hand.

"What? I was talking about how happy painting makes you feel."

Sara placed a large notebook in front of Raphael and placed her hand upon it. "First tell me what you want to drink and then you can look."

"I'll have a sweet tea," Raphael said.

"Me, too," Toby added.

Sara rushed off to get their drinks.

Raphael handed the book to Toby.

"Thanks!" Toby flipped open the book and took his time studying the drawings. "How long has Sara been doing this?" Toby asked.

"When she was old enough to hold a crayon. We could tell at age two there was something special about her because she colored a page from a coloring book completely within the lines. She worked on it for over thirty minutes, choosing colors. We framed it." Raj pointed across the diner to a picture hanging on the far wall.

Sara returned with their drinks. "Here you go." She set the drinks in front of each man. "Have you decided on what you want to eat?"

"That's my cue to get back in the kitchen." Raj moved back to the kitchen area.

Raphael nodded. "I'll have your special burger with fries."

"That sounds good. I'll have that, too." Toby winked at Sara as he handed her the menus. Sara blushed, then headed back to the kitchen.

Toby looked through the book of Sara's images again. The detail was exquisite. Some of the images were of famous people and some were ordinary people. There were images in black and white and some in color. There must have been over a hundred.

Sara returned with their food and Toby closed the book.

"Sara, I love these images. I wish I could ask you more about some of them," he said. Toby handed her the notebook.

"How about after dinner?" Sara asked.

Toby glanced at Raphael.

"We can stay tonight. I'll set up camp out back, if that's okay with Sara's father?" Raphael glanced at her for approval.

"I'll ask," she said. Sara rushed back to the kitchen.

"There is something so familiar about these images," Toby said. "It's like I've seen them before."

"Perhaps you have," Raphael said, biting into his burger.

Toby felt excited to speak to Sara. She was beautiful, but somehow seemed familiar to him. And why were her images familiar as well?

After their meal, Raphael and Raj went outside to set up camp.

Sara wiped down the table while Toby used the restroom. By the time he returned, Sara had the notebook out on the table and two cups of coffee.

Toby sat down and Sara sat beside him. Toby smiled at her, flattered by her nearness. "I wanted to ask you about a couple of the images," Toby began.

"Sure." Sara sat with her hands folded in front of her.

Toby turned the page to two animal images. "These look so familiar. How old were you when you did these?"

"I was seven when I drew these." She reached over him and pulled the images out of the notebook, turning them over. The dates were on the back.

Toby flipped to a couple more images and Sara pulled those out as well.

"I was eight when I did those." Something fell out from between the images.

Toby picked it up. It was a photo of a girl and a boy. "That's me when I was eight! And this is the little girl who gave me this." Toby pulled out the necklace he wore under his shirt.

Sara studied Toby's necklace, then pulled out a similar

necklace from under her shirt that said 'Friends'. "That's me in that picture!"

"I've been thinking of you all these years," Toby said.

"Me, too!"

The two of them hugged.

"Let me show you something." Sara flipped ahead in the book and stopped at an image of two kids. "What do you think?"

"Is that us?"

"Yes!"

"I love it! That's another one I had a question about. No wonder it was so familiar."

Sara pulled out another image of her and a man with no face. "Now I can finish this."

"It's like we were meant to be," Toby said.

"You think so?"

Toby lifted Sara's chin. "Yes." Then he kissed her gently on the lips. She kissed him back and a surge of energy rushed through him.

"Did you feel that?" Sara asked.

"Yes, I did."

"I've never felt that before, have you?" she asked.

"No. This is a first for me, too."

"I had hoped all these years to see you again," she said.

8

———

Raj rushed into the diner. "Raphael had an emergency. He will return tomorrow."

"Tomorrow?" Toby was stunned. Tomorrow was Tuesday. Raphael had planned to go to California first. This would throw off his job interview for this Thursday. And where would he stay? He had no vehicle and no money except for gas. All his things were on the truck. "Did he take the truck?"

"Of course! I insist you stay with us." Raj said. "I have some clothes that might fit you."

Toby blinked a few times. Things happened fast around Raphael. "Uh, yes. Thank you."

"We have a couple hours before closing time," Sara said. "You can help me clean up!"

"Sure." What could he say? He was at the mercy of other people. He needed to call Mr. Haynes and reschedule the interview. He picked up his phone but noticed it was after 6pm. Mr. Haynes wouldn't be in the office until the next morning. The call would have to wait.

Sara stood and held her hand out. "Come with me and I'll show you what we do here."

Toby took Sara's hand and let her lead him around the small diner.

"It's been slow today, so I've wiped all the tables but this one." She handed a dish rag to Toby. "While you wipe our table, I'll refill the shakers."

Toby wiped down the table and watched as Sara refilled each salt shaker before starting on the pepper shakers. Toby wiped down the bar top while Sara set all the shakers back on the tables.

"Come back here," Sara said. She walked around to the back of the bar and washed her hands. Toby followed suit then helped her restock the napkin holders.

While he placed all of them on the tables, Sara took all the ketchup and mustard containers to the back of the bar where she replenished each container and placed them in the refrigerator next to the mayo containers.

"Do you want to sweep or mop?" she asked.

"Hmm. Which do you hate doing?" Toby asked her.

"Mopping."

"Then I'll mop."

Sara locked the door to the diner and started running the water in the mop bucket for Toby. "Put in a quarter cup of the cleaner when it's almost full," she said.

Sara put the chairs on the table tops and swept the floors.

Toby waited for the water. This wasn't so bad. He felt he was earning his keep for the night. But what happened that Raphael had to leave in such a hurry?

When he finished mopping, Sara showed him where to put the empty bucket and mop.

"You're finished in record time!" Miriam said.

"Go on upstairs. We'll join you shortly," Raj said.

There was a door to their apartment outside the diner, between the gas station bathrooms. Sara locked the diner from outside and unlocked the apartment door. A stairway took them up one floor.

"How do you like living above the diner?" Toby asked.

"It's the only life I've ever known."

"Is it just you and your parents, then?"

"Well, until recently, we had Karen working for us on the busiest days. She was not a nice person so my parents let her go. We have Jake, who runs the gas station, and his son helps him on the weekends. They live in town."

"How far is the nearest town?"

"About five miles."

"So, what do you do for fun around here?"

"I read a lot, draw pictures, and play board games with my parents. Once in a while, we go to town for a movie."

"Sounds like what I used to do with my parents," Toby said. "Except the drawing part."

"So, what changed for you?"

"I went to college and got a degree in teaching. I have an interview this week for a job in Arizona teaching elementary school."

"That sounds exciting."

"Yes. I'm a little excited and worried at the same time."

"Why are you worried?"

"I may not make it to the interview. I'll have to call and reschedule it. My car broke down on the highway and Raphael rescued me. I feel so helpless at the mercy of other people."

"Have a seat." She showed him to the sofa. "I'll get us some tea."

"Thanks." Toby glanced around the living room and noticed the images of Sara as a young child and a growing teen. There were pictures everywhere. It reminded him of his home and the images of himself growing up.

When Sara handed him the tea, her parents walked in and joined them.

"We brought some cake from the diner. Anyone up for a board game tonight?" Miriam asked.

Before long, the four of them played Monopoly until Raj announced it was time for bed.

He showed Toby to a guest room and gave him a change of clothes. Sara showed Toby where the bathroom was.

"Goodnight Sara," he said. He gave her hand a squeeze.

Sara stood on tiptoe and gave him a chaste kiss.

9

———

Raj called out to everyone early the next morning. "Time to awaken! It's a new day."

Toby bolted up in his bed, rubbing his eyes. He glanced around the room, trying to remember where he was and how he got there. He found his phone but it was dead.

"My charger was on the truck!" How was he going to call Mr. Haynes? He didn't know his phone number; it was on his cell phone, which was dead. He ran his hand through his hair. He hoped Raphael got back soon. After changing clothes, he headed to the living room and joined Sara's family.

Raj led the family in a short prayer for a good and prosperous day and then they headed to the diner.

Toby helped Sara take the chairs off the tables and then wiped the tables once more while Sara set the condiments out.

Raj cooked up breakfast for everyone and Miriam served them at the bar.

While they ate, Toby asked questions to break the ice.

"Where did you two meet?"

"We met in school," Raj said.

"Yes, we hit it off right from the start," Miriam added.

"Did you always work here?"

"No. I worked in a restaurant in town. When this property went up for sale, I bought it."

"Has it always been a diner?"

"No. It was a gas station only. I ran it myself for a while, adding a small store. People kept stopping and asking for a diner. I thought I could do that, too."

"But he couldn't do it alone, so he asked me to join him in this adventure," Miriam added.

"And the rest is history," Sara said.

Toby helped Sara with the customers; while she took the orders, he got their drinks and brought their food. He felt they worked well as a team.

When they had a slow period, Sara showed Toby how to draw simple images.

"You're good at this, Sara. Have you ever thought about teaching others to draw?"

"No. I never had that thought. Do you think I could?"

"Yes, you're patient with me so I think you could teach others as well."

As the day wound down, Toby realized he still hadn't called Mr. Haynes. "Have you heard anything from Raphael?" Toby asked Raj.

"All he told me was he would be here sometime today."

That was vague and he needed to get information to Mr. Haynes, but how would he do it?

"You look worried, Toby," Sara said. She touched his arm.

Just her touch seemed to soothe him. "Remember the interview I told you about?"

"Yes."

"Well, if Raphael doesn't come back, I won't make it to the interview." He took Sara by the hand and led her outside. The diner was empty at the moment.

"My father had an accident and needs financial help. I thought by taking this interview, I could support myself and my parents. But my father sent me on a quest to find his fortune in California. There's someone there who might be able to help him, but I have to find him first. I did some research on my phone and narrowed down my search, but without my car or my phone, I'm useless. I hope Raphael makes it back soon. I can charge my phone and get in touch with Mr. Haynes to reschedule the interview. I really don't want to mess up this opportunity."

"If Raphael said he would be here, then he will be here. He is a man of his word."

Toby moved a brown curl framing Sara's face and tucked it behind her ear.

"I think we have a lot in common, Sara. It feels like we were meant to be."

"I feel it, too."

"You know, I feel more connected to you than any girl I've ever known."

Sara smiled.

"Once I get through with my interview and finish this quest, I'd like to marry you.

"I would love to marry you," Sara said.

Toby touched a finger to her lips. "If I get the job, that will determine where we'll live."

"I will follow you anywhere," she whispered.

Toby kissed Sara passionately and she returned the kiss.

10

"Ahem!" Sara's mother cleared her throat. "It's closing time."

"We're getting married!" Toby announced.

Sara's mother made the sign of the cross. She grabbed Sara by the arm. "Come with me."

Confused, Toby followed them back inside but ran into Raphael and Raj.

"Miriam told us the good news! I will go and fetch the priest," Raj said. He hurried away.

"What? I was going to wait until we returned from California," Toby said.

"Come with me," Raphael said. He escorted Toby outside. The sun was low in the western sky. Raphael handed the baggy with the heart, liver, and gall to Toby.

"Don't forget what I said about the heart and liver," Raphael said.

"Are you serious?"

"Yes, your life depends on it."

"What are you talking about?"

"Sara has been married three times, but each bridegroom killed himself on their wedding night before consummating the marriage."

"What? Why didn't you tell me this?"

"It wasn't necessary until now. She is cursed by the evil spirit, Asmodeus. Do what I told you with the heart and liver and in the morning, you will be a happily married man."

"And the gall?"

"Save it. It has healing properties."

"Everything seems so...surreal. This is all happening too fast," Toby said.

"You have known of Sara a long time. You were meant to be together. Tonight, you will be married. I will go to California and find Zacarias and bring him here."

The priest rushed in with Raj and Jake, the man who worked for Raj at the gas station. Raj ushered everyone upstairs to the family's living quarters. Raphael and Jake stood as witnesses near the priest. Toby stood near the fireplace with the priest. Miriam walked in and stood next to Raj on the side where Toby stood. Then Sara walked in between all of them. She was dressed in a simple white dress. Her brown hair was pinned up with a few curls framing her face.

Toby was mesmerized by her beauty. She came and stood next to Toby. She had some flowers in her hair that made her look even more beautiful.

The ceremony was simple. Toby had never thought about how his wedding would go, but he liked this one. Miriam and Raj hugged him afterward and welcomed him into the family. Raphael and Jake shook his hand, congratulating him. The priest had each of them sign the forms to verify the ceremony.

Miriam brought in some cake from the diner and a

bottle of champagne, which they drank to toast the couple's future.

"I'll be back as soon as I find Zacarias," Raphael said. He left and so did Jake and the priest. Raj and Miriam escorted the couple to their wedding chamber, which looked just like the room Toby slept in the night before.

Toby and Sara stood in the room with Raj and Miriam. He held Sara's hands in his, then dropped her hands and cupped her face in his hands, kissing her. She reciprocated.

Toby remembered what Raphael told him and pulled the baggy out of his pocket. He went to the burning candle on the dresser. There was a small container with incense sitting in front of the candle. He lit the incense and placed the heart and liver on the small container and burned them as well.

"What are you doing?" Sara asked.

"Raphael told me to do this. He said you were cursed by Asmodeus."

A cold breeze rushed through the room, throwing open the window. Sara put her arms around Toby. "What's happening?"

"Sara, let's pray." Toby knelt down and Sara did the same. Raj and Miriam knelt down behind them.

"Bless you, oh God, forever and ever. Let the heavens bless you and all things you have made, forever and ever. It was you who created Adam and Eve to be his help and support. Be kind enough to have pity on Sara and me and bring us to old age together," Toby said.

"Amen," Sara said.

"Amen," Raj and Miriam added. The two stood and left the room, leaving Sara and Toby alone.

Asmodeus fled through the air the moment the reek of the

liver and heart found his nostrils. But he didn't get far before Raphael bound and shackled him and sent him back to hell.

Toby slowly removed the flowers from Sara's hair and pulled out the hairpins, letting her long hair fall around her shoulders. He pulled her close, kissing her more passionately, but felt her tremble.

"What's wrong?"

"I've never gotten this far with any of my...grooms."

"We were meant to be together, Sara. Asmodeus will never bother us again." He hugged her tight. Sara clung to Toby until her trembling stopped completely. When she felt safe in his arms, he carried her to the bed and they consummated their marriage.

11

———

Raphael went on to California and found Anthony Zacarias.

"Come with me to the wedding feast of the son of Tobias Flint," Raphael said.

"Tobias Flint? I haven't heard from him in years. How is he doing?"

"He had an accident and is in need of his investment monies."

"Oh, my! He left his money with me these past twenty-three years and I've invested it over and over. He is a wealthy man. I should like to meet his son and see Tobias once more. I need to settle his accounts but I can follow you back in the morning."

"That will be fine. I'll be back in the morning."

Later that night, Sara's parents prayed.

"Oh God, please spare Toby's life and may he and Sara live long and healthy lives, bearing many children," Raj said.

"Amen," Miriam said.

Raj and Miriam stood and went to bed, leaving the fate

of their daughter and her new husband in God's hands. They wanted their daughter to be happy and they knew the diner was not where she wanted to spend the rest of her life.

Meanwhile, in Tennessee, Tobias sat in his chair, twiddling his thumbs. "It has been several days and we've not heard a word from Toby. I fear something has happened."

"Have faith, Tobias. You must leave everything in God's hands. He has never let you down." Anna touched his cheek.

"You are right, Anna." He reached a hand out to her and she grabbed it.

"You have been kind to others when they were down. Now it's your turn, Tobias. Be patient and have faith." She kissed his cheek and went on to work.

The next morning, Raj and Miriam were opening the diner.

"I should go and prepare a grave," he said.

"We prayed last night. Have you lost your faith already?"

"We have been cursed."

"Don't you remember Toby burned the heart and liver to send away the demon?"

"Yes, but—"

"No buts! We are done with the demon. I feel it."

Sara and Toby came downstairs and into the diner. Sara beamed when she saw her parents.

"Bless you! Bless you both!" Miriam rushed to hug them.

"Praise God! We have a son-in-law!" Raj said as he hugged them both.

Sara put on her apron and handed one to Toby. "You are family now, so get to work," she teased.

Sara and her mother prepared the dining room, while

her father prepared breakfast. Toby helped in the kitchen area.

"Raphael went to Media to fetch Anthony Zacarias. When he returns tonight, we will have a wedding feast. I will invite everyone!" Raj said as he patted Toby on the back.

When Jake arrived, Raj briefed him on the coming events.

"Dad's been out there for a while, now," Sara said. She sat at a window booth next to Toby and across from Miriam as they ate their own breakfast. She saw her father shake hands with Jake. He had been a faithful employee all these years.

"I will miss you and Dad," Sara said. "But not this place. It never felt like I belonged here."

Toby patted her knee. "You can still visit them," he said.

"Toby has an interview for a teaching job in Arizona," she told her mother.

"Really? What will you teach?" Miriam asked.

"Elementary school. All subjects, I guess, unless they have some other plans for me."

"That is a great plan," she said. "Arizona is not far from here."

"After my interview, I will return home to help my father. The bank is about to foreclose on his house."

"Oh, no!"

"He had an accident that made it difficult to walk without a cane and then he lost his sight. He was a professor at a university in middle Tennessee until recently. They laid him off because he was out so long."

"Will you return here after that?" Miriam asked.

"That all depends on the interview and the bank, but I would like to come back for a visit." Toby squeezed Sara's hand. "We haven't had time to discuss anything." He glanced at her.

"Yes, you need to have that discussion and let us know where you will be staying, so we can visit you, too."

"You and Dad never leave this place," Sara said.

"One day, we will retire and then we will."

The day dragged on. Sara and Toby helped clean the place up for closing time, while Raj cooked up a storm for the wedding feast.

"Go and get ready for your guests," Raj said. "The wedding feast will be soon."

Sara and Toby headed upstairs to shower and change.

12

———

Raj and Miriam busied themselves with decorating the diner for the wedding party. They hung some streamers and balloons, set the food out like a buffet and turned on the music.

People trickled in, congratulating Raj and Miriam for their new son-in-law.

Sara and Toby made their entrance, dressed casually. There were gifts on the tables.

"What's all this?" Toby asked.

"Wedding gifts!" Miriam said.

"Ah, Raphael is here," Raj said as he went to greet him.

"This place is packed," Toby said, looking around.

"Yes, I didn't know Dad had so many friends," Sara said.

Raphael and an older gentleman made their way to Toby and Sara.

"You must be Toby," the older man said.

"Yes, sir." Toby offered his hand and the two shook hands.

"I'm Anthony Zacarias. Here's something for your father." He produced a check with a lot of zeros.

"Wow! That's a lot of money," Toby said.

"That's a fraction of his wealth. Your father trusted me when no one else would. I will come to visit him later this month with the rest of his money."

Toby wrote down his father's address and phone number for Anthony.

"This is for the two of you, to help you get started." Anthony handed Toby another check for $1,000.00 and a certificate showing an investment in mutual funds.

"Wow, thank you!"

"Allow me to re-invest your money as it earns and you will have a fortune as well."

"Yes, definitely!" Toby shook hands with Anthony once more.

Sara beamed as people shook her hand and wished her well.

As the night wore on, people left and Sara and Toby picked up plates and containers, taking them to the kitchen.

"No, no. We'll get this," Miriam insisted. "Raphael says you have an interview soon. Go get your rest. You have a long drive ahead of you."

The next day, Toby, Sara, and Raphael set out for Arizona. Toby charged his phone to navigate to Mr. Haynes' office and went over the notes he made when he first met Mr. Haynes.

"Tell me why I should hire you?" Sara asked him.

"Because I'm honest, trustworthy, I pay attention to details, I think outside the box and I love kids," he said.

He and Sara practiced while Raphael drove. Finally, Raphael pulled into a parking lot in front of the school board building.

Toby called Mr. Haynes to verify they were in the right place. He headed up to the building while Sara remained in the truck with Raphael.

"What will you do with yourself now that you no longer work at the diner?" Raphael asked her.

"I hadn't thought about it. Everything happened so quickly. I guess I could get a job somewhere and draw or paint on the side."

"Or maybe you could get a job drawing or painting?"

Sara cocked her head. What kind of job would that be?

"Let's see those images Toby looked at the other day," Raphael asked.

Sara searched for her notebook and couldn't find it.

"Did you pack the notebook?" Raphael asked.

"I distinctly remember carrying it in here."

Toby opened the cab door. He gestured to Sara. "Mr. Haynes wants to meet the artist who drew these pictures." Toby raised the notebook for both of them to see.

"Did you get the job?" Sara asked.

"Yes, and they need an art teacher as well. Maybe you can work at the school part-time while taking classes to become an art teacher."

Sara jumped down from the cab and leapt into Toby's arms. She kissed his face and they went to speak to the superintendent together.

Afterwards, the two of them returned to Raphael's truck and the three of them headed back to middle Tennessee. After many stops for coffee and a stopover in Oklahoma, Raphael pulled up to Tobias' house.

13

"Come and see this!" Anna said to Tobias.

"You know I can't see. Tell me about it," he said.

"An eighteen-wheeler just pulled up to the house," she said.

"A semi?"

"Yes! Three people are getting out. Oh, one looks like Toby! It is Toby!" Anna pulled the door open and ran out to greet them.

"Toby, you are safe! We were so worried about you. You haven't called us. We tried calling you but your phone went to voicemail."

Toby hugged his mother. "I'm sorry, Mom. My phone was dead and everything happened so fast. This is Raphael, the man who helped me find Anthony Zacarias."

Raphael reached out and shook Anna's hand. "So nice to meet you, Ms. Flint."

"You, too. Thank you for helping my son."

"And this is my wife, Sara." Toby gestured to Sara.

"Your wife!" Anna hugged Sara. "Welcome to the family. We have a lot to talk about, don't we?"

"Yes, we do."

"Come, come. Tobias is anxious for us to come inside."
She ushered everyone into the house. Once inside, Anna
explained everything to Tobias.

Tobias was happy to hear his son's voice. Toby hugged
his father. "You have nothing to worry about, Dad. The Lord
has answered your prayers."

A tear fell down Tobias' cheek. "We must celebrate your
safe return and your marriage to Sara."

"And my new job," Toby added.

"Yes. When do you start?"

"In a few weeks. Teachers have to be there a month
before the students for planning. That reminds me." Toby
pulled the baggy with the fish gall out of his pocket. He
mashed the gall inside the baggy and then pulled some out
to smear across his father's eyes.

"Oh, that smells awful," Tobias said. "What is it?"

"Fish gall," Raphael answered. "When it dries, blow
on it."

Toby waited, then blew across his father's eyes.

"Now, remove the film," Raphael instructed him. Toby
carefully peeled the film off his father's eyes.

Tobias' eyes fluttered open. "I can see! I see you!"

Tobias hugged Toby and then Raphael. "Thank you!"
Then he hugged Anna. "Praise God! I can see!"

"Thank you, Jesus!" Anna said.

"Praise God!" Toby said.

"We must pay you for your help, Raphael," Tobias said.

"No, I am Raphael, one of the seven who stands before
God. I was sent here to answer Sara's and Tobias' prayers."

Tobias, Toby, Sara and Anna all knelt down in Raphael's
presence.

"Praise be to God!" Tobias said. Toby, Sara and Anna
repeated "Praise be to God!"

"All praise and honor to almighty God, forever and ever," Raphael said. And then, he was gone.

The four of them jumped up to look for him, but he was truly gone.

Toby glanced out the window. "Hey, his truck is gone but my Volkswagen is in its place."

Sara and Toby ran out to the VW bug to find all their belongings still inside the car. Toby's keys were still in the ignition and when he turned the key, the car started as if nothing was wrong.

END

BETWEEN HEAVEN AND EARTH

BOOK 2 IN THE ANGEL CHRONICLES SERIES

Here's an excerpt from book 2 in the Angel Chronicles Series, **Between Heaven and Earth.** *I hope you enjoy it.*

María Rojas looked up and down the alley to make sure no one watched before sliding the lid open and peering inside her favorite dumpster.

Good. No rats.

She scrunched her nose as the faint, pungent aroma of rotting food assaulted her senses. Her dumpster had once been used by neighboring restaurants, although lately it had been taken over by local offices for paper trash. But it was an odor she could live with, considering her choices.

Pushing off from the sturdy can beside the large metal container, she hauled herself up through the opening and dropped onto a pile of cardboard boxes broken down inside the dumpster.

She had slept in worse places, but tonight she would sleep well.

She made the sign of the cross and whispered her nightly prayer.

"Angel of God, my guardian dear, to whom God's love

commits me here, ever this day be at my side, to light, to guard, to rule and guide. Amen."

Making the sign of the cross once more, she curled up on the cardboard pallet and covered her face with her hat.

Early October, the nights cooled down in Pensacola. She hugged herself to keep warm. If she didn't get off the streets soon, the nights would become unbearably cold.

Patting the outside of her coat, she made certain her earnings were still inside. Tomorrow, after work, she would make a deposit.

One day soon she would have enough money saved to pay off Mr. Turner and get her apartment and belongings back. Then she would see about returning to nursing school. Her instructors gave her 'incompletes' to finish the term, but she would have to make up all those classes before moving on.

Even with the extra hours Mr. Brodsky had given her at the Greasy Spoon, the pay wasn't enough to get her out of debt. Maybe he would let her become a server as well as dishwasher. With her skills, she had limited choices. She forced the thoughts from her mind, and gradually dozed off.

Hours later, she awoke to the sound of footsteps running down the alley toward her.

"Hey, old man, what's your hurry?" a male voice called out.

Her pulse quickened as she sat up and listened. Peering through a rust hole in the dumpster, she saw three men. One of them was someone she had seen at the Soup Kitchen. The three men were about the same six feet in height.

She moved closer to get a better look. Although two of

them had their backs to her, she saw from the street light they wore blue jeans with casual suit jackets. One man had on running shoes with a lightning bolt design on the side. The other man wore loafers.

She recognized the old man as Joe Blue, when he threw his hands up in the air. "I don't want any trouble," he said. His eyes widened, a worried look on his face.

Her heart rate shot up. That didn't sound good. Oh, Lord, help him.

"It's too late for that, old man. You've already seen too much," the man in the running shoes said.

The other man reached into his pocket, pulled out a taser and stuck Joe with it. Joe jerked a few times then fell back against the wall before sliding to the ground.

She leaned closer to the side of the dumpster and saw the man in the running shoes pull a hypodermic needle out of his pocket.

He pulled back on the syringe, while inserting the needle into a bottle.

The other man held Joe's arm while the first one injected him with the liquid.

"N—," she tried to scream, but her vocal chords wouldn't cooperate.

Panic set in. She had to stop them. She brought her hand up to hit the inside of the dumpster, when someone clamped a hand over her mouth and pulled her back, pinning her arms to her sides. Startled, she jerked, banging the wall of her makeshift sleeping quarters with her foot. Then a leg wrapped over her hips, preventing her from moving. Her heart pounded furiously.

The two men turned and looked at the dumpster. Her heart skipped a beat as she held her breath. *Don't come over here.*

Two rats scurried out the top of the container.

Wincing at the sight, she swallowed hard.

Where did **they** come from? And who was holding her?

She struggled to free herself when a sense of peace flowed through her suddenly, as if she, too, had been injected with something potent.

"Damn rats," one of the men said.

"They give me the creeps," the other one said, turning back to Joe.

"What about him?"

"We'll take him with us. I know just the place to leave him." He bent down and picked up Joe under the shoulders.

"Grab his feet."

Where were they going with Joe Blue?

The hand against her mouth loosened, as well as the arm around her waist and the leg over her hip. The warmth of the body behind her left immediately. She pulled away and spun around on her side to see who shared the small quarters with her. In the dark, she made out the shape of a man, much larger than her small five-foot-two-inch frame, with hair that hung down below his ears.

"How...did you get in here?" she asked.

"Never mind that, we have to leave now," he said. He ran a hand through his hair. He stood up, put his hands on the top of the dumpster and leapt over the side of the container.

María may have seen three men tonight, but he had seen six, counting the two evil spirits, the two criminals, the old man and his Guardian Angel.

The spirits were so intent on their evil deed they failed to notice his presence, or they would have alerted the two moles.

He held his hands up to help María down from the top of the container.

"Hey!" She leaned over the edge. "How did you make that jump in one movement?" She hiked a leg over the side.

He caught her under the armpits and pulled her toward him. Her hands pressed against his shoulders as he slowly brought her to the ground. She was light and pleasing to hold and the touch of her hands against his bare skin felt warm and comforting.

Earlier, when he had his hand across her mouth, her lips felt soft and her warm breath moistened his fingers. The sensation that ran through him when he cradled her body against his was unexpected, but he remembered it from before.

Before? If he had never manifested in the flesh, how could he remember that strange and pleasant sensation? Now, he would never forget it.

María scratched her head as she looked him up and down. A smile escaped his lips when he noticed how she tried to look mad.

"Who are you and what were you doing in my dumpster?" María demanded, her hands on her hips.

"Your dumpster? I thought it belonged to the City of Pensacola." He turned and walked away from her. He had forgotten how amusing she could be, but he had to get her to safety before the thugs returned.

"I asked you a question," she demanded, following him.

"The name's Mike," he said over his shoulder, and quickened his pace. Hopefully, she would follow without further questions.

"Hey, wait up. What happened to Joe Blue?" She trotted after him.

"They took his body. They'll dump it under the overpass

for someone to find in the morning." María's inquisitiveness never ceased to entertain him.

"How do you *know* that?" she asked, taking longer strides to keep up.

"I know a lot of things." He stopped and turned toward her. "Right now, we need to leave this place." He could hear the car slowly moving toward them.

"But shouldn't we call the cops or something?" she protested.

"It wouldn't do any good. The man is dead, and his spirit moved on. They wouldn't believe you anyway, because you don't know where the body is."

"Well...if you know, couldn't you tell them?" she said, poking his chest.

"They can't see me. Only you can see me."

"What are you talking about?" She put her hands on her hips and looked up at him.

The car moved closer to the alley, as the sound of rubber tires crushing against asphalt grew louder. He reached his arms around María and held her tight. The sensation of her body against his stunned him momentarily, but he thought of the Waffle House and was there instantly.

"How did you...we...get here?" She craned her neck to look up at this amazingly good-looking guy.

"I'll explain everything," he said, releasing her. He held the door of the Waffle House open as she walked past him and went inside. Immediately, she missed the warmth of his touch.

Who was this guy, and why did she feel safe around him?

Inside, there were two people in a booth, as well as a

waitress and a cook. Dazed, she found a booth on the far side of the restaurant, near a window, and slipped into the seat. The man sat across from her.

"Okay, who are you, and why are we here?" she asked. Looking at him, she crossed her arms over her chest. He had a lot to answer for, that was certain.

Handsome in an elegant sort of way, he looked nothing like any of the men she had seen on campus. His dark-brown eyes and golden-brown skin had a healthy glow. His black, thick brows, matching his wavy hair, drew her to his face, but the dimple on his left cheek held her gaze. He was gorgeous.

Oh, and those muscular shoulders and bare arms had seen a lot of workouts. His forearms were covered with black curly hair and his full lips and round nose made him look like a guy who enjoyed life and knew how to have fun.

"Hey, there. My name's Susan. Can I get you both something to drink?" The waitress interrupted her thoughts. Susan was in her forties with thick, grayish-brown hair pulled back in a pony tail with bangs.

Mike's gaze snapped toward the woman.

"Can you see me?" he asked her, his eyes wide.

"Of course, I can see you, honey, I'm not blind." She lowered her bifocals. "And you're not bad-looking either," she said, putting her hands on her hips. "What in the world are you two wearing?" Susan looked them both over.

"Um…we've been to a costume party," María lied. She was just as anxious to find out why Mike was wearing an ancient Roman soldier's uniform, complete with a breast-plate. Although, her reason for wearing a man's suit was to hide the fact she was a woman living on the streets, she wasn't about to tell a stranger that.

Mike looked at her and raised an eyebrow.

"You know, you look really familiar somehow. Have you been in here before?" Susan asked him, in a raspy voice.

"I don't think so," Mike said, looking at Susan. "This is my first time here."

"I'm pretty bad at remembering names, but I sure can remember a face. And I've seen you in here before."

Mike leaned back and managed to smile. "Maybe I have a twin somewhere," he said.

"Was your father on the police force?" Susan asked, looking down at him.

"My father? Uh, no...I...no." Mike shook his head slowly, then sat back in his seat.

"Hmmm," Susan said, chewing on the end of her pen. Her tired greenish-brown eyes studied him.

"Could we have some coffee with cream and sugar, please?" Mike asked.

"Sure, honey. I'll be right back." She turned and left.

María leaned forward and whispered loudly, "I thought you said no one could see you?"

"Well, I've never manifested in the flesh before. I didn't think anyone could see me," he said, closing his eyes. Then he disappeared.

"Hey, where'd he go?" Susan asked, setting down the coffee and creamer.

"Um...bathroom," María lied, chewing on her bottom lip.

Susan looked around, then pulled out her pad and pen. "Are you ready to order, honey?"

"Not yet. Maybe in a few minutes," she said.

"Okay. I'll check back, then." Susan returned to the grill area.

"Can you see me now?" Mike asked.

"No, but I can hear you." María reached across the table

and moved her hand through the space he had just occupied. "How are you doing that?"

Mike reappeared and caught her hand in his. "I'm your Guardian Angel."

She yanked her hand away and dropped back into her seat. "What?"

Mike leaned across the table and spoke in a whisper. "I've been your Guardian Angel since the day you were born."

María's mouth dropped open. A million questions formed in her mind instantly. "Am I going to die?" Her heart rate shot up at the thought.

"Yes, but not for a very long time." Mike leaned forward. "You were about to scream when you witnessed that murder. It wasn't your time to go, so I had to intervene, or you would have been next."

She caught her throat with her hand. "I...couldn't scream. I tried but—" She remembered the scene vividly.

"I stopped you, then realized you were going to bang on the dumpster. I had to take drastic measures. My mission is to protect you from all harm."

"How did you know I was going to bang on the dumpster?"

"I can hear your thoughts."

María blinked as her hand dropped away from her throat. "All of them?"

Mike nodded. "Since the day you were born."

She swallowed hard, recalling her recent thoughts about him. "Can you turn it off?"

"I'm afraid not."

She had a lot of thoughts--questions--running through her mind. "When do you have to...go back?"

"Go back?" he asked, raising an eyebrow.

"You know, to heaven?"

"I guess when it's your time to go. I'm with you for the long haul."

"You mean until I die?"

Mike nodded.

"Well, are you two ready to order?" Maria jumped at Susan's approach.

"Hi." He smiled at Susan. "I guess I'll have the All-Star Special."

Susan scribbled on her pad, then froze. She looked at Mike. "You used to be a regular here." She pointed at him with her pen. "And you used to sit at this same booth and ordered the same thing every time you came in. I remember now." Susan turned and called out. "Bobby, come here."

The cook approached the table, wiping his hands on his apron. Mike looked at Maria and offered a half smile, raising an eyebrow.

"Look at him, Bobby. Who does he remind you of?"

Bobby stared at Mike. "You look like the cop who used to come in here with his partner every Sunday while on patrol." Bobby turned toward Susan. "But that was—"

"Twenty-three years ago." Susan finished.

"You must have me confused with someone else," Mike said.

"Your partner still comes in here from time to time. I'll ask him," Susan said.

"That's a good idea," Mike said, raising both eyebrows. "Now, how about that special?"

"One All-Star Special coming up. How about you, honey, do you want anything to eat?" Susan looked at María.

"I...uh...I'll have the same thing, please," she said, looking at Susan.

"I'll be right back," Susan said, pushing Bobby back toward the kitchen.

She glanced at the clock. It was after four a.m. She

would have to be at work in a couple of hours. She felt for her pocket with the cash in it.

"I hate to ask this, but who's paying for this meal?" She poured the creamer into her cup of coffee.

"You'll have to, since I don't carry any money," Mike said, taking a sip of his coffee.

"You know how long I've been saving?" She stirred in the sugar. It had been two months since she had been locked out of her apartment.

"Yes, and if you hadn't dropped out of college, you would have made a lot more money in the near future."

María glared at him. "Where were you when I had to make that decision?" With no place to live, where was she supposed to go? Mr. Turner had everything she owned in storage, including her books. She had no money to replace them, let alone pay her back rent.

"I tried to guide you in the other direction, but you didn't listen."

María sipped her coffee. How could she have done otherwise? After her father's untimely death from cancer two years earlier had drained their savings, her mother was forced to sell the only home Maria had ever known to pay off his debt. Without her mother's income, she had no place to live, and no way to continue school. "Well, maybe you didn't try hard enough."

Mike put his coffee down. "What is that supposed to mean?"

"How long have you been an angel, anyway? Did you have any other assignments before you were my Guardian Angel?"

"I...honestly don't remember," he said, sipping his coffee.

"Here you go," Susan said, setting the All-Star Specials

down in front of them. "I'll get you some more coffee." She turned back to the kitchen.

"Wow, that's a lot of food," María said. She hadn't eaten this much food in a long time...since her mother had been well.

"Eat up. You won't get to eat again until late today, remember?" Mike said.

Susan returned with the coffee and poured some for her. She turned to pour some for Mike. "I thought you wanted cream and sugar?" she asked him, looking at his half-full cup.

"No, I drink mine black," he said.

"That's right." Susan nodded as she locked gazes with Mike, then left.

"How do you know you drink your coffee black?" María asked him. "Have you ever had coffee before? And do angels eat and drink?"

"I...no...angels don't eat and drink, unless we take human form."

"Well, the way you said it was like you'd been drinking coffee for years. How do you know you won't like it with cream and sugar?"

"I don't, I mean...I like mine black."

"Yeah, right." She poked her eggs with her fork. She couldn't understand why she wanted to be mad at this man. He hadn't done anything wrong to deserve her anger. This was the first hot breakfast she'd had in a week and it tasted good, but the cost would set her back on reaching her goal.

Mike watched her eat while new thoughts ran through his head. He took another sip of coffee. The smells and tastes that he experienced sent thousands of images through his mind. Images of things he remembered from a past that he didn't know he had. And her questions brought new thoughts to his mind as well. For instance, the first taste of coffee felt so natural to his tongue, yet he remembered tasting coffee that was too strong as well as too weak. He remembered coffee that was exquisite as well as downright nasty. But if this was his first taste, then where did these memories come from? And how did he know he liked it black?

Mike tasted the eggs. Boy, they were good. He really missed this breakfast. His hand froze over the sausage. How could he miss something he never had? And why did it taste so familiar? The hash browns were good and crispy, just the way he liked them. But how did he know that?

He cut his sausage patties up and folded them into his last slice of toast and made a sandwich out of it. He stared at the food in his hand. This was all so familiar to him. Did he actually come here with a partner as Susan suggested? Had he been a cop at one time? And why did he even pick this place? María had never come here before, and how did he know this place was even here?

"So now what happens?" María asked, finishing her last piece of toast.

"We wait until you have to be at work."

"That's not for another hour and a half," she said, glancing at the clock. "What do we do in the meantime?" She sat back in her seat, her arms crossed over her chest.

"I can answer any questions you might have," he said.

"Really?"

He nodded.

"What else do angels do besides read people's minds?"

"We protect and guard you, give guidance, in other words, everything you pray and ask us to do, providing it's God's will for you, but I can't interfere with free will."

"Can you see into the future...my future?"

"Sometimes."

"Well...what does mine look like?"

"Your destiny was to become a nurse, but you changed that with your decision to drop out of college."

"Why didn't you help me with that decision? You know why I made it." She pointed at him as she lowered her voice.

He had tried desperately to convince her to stay in school, but her mother's death pulled her away from logical thinking. "Yes, I know why, but you didn't ask for my help then. You made that decision on your own." María hadn't been tuned in to listening to her conscience, which was his only way of speaking to her as a spirit being.

María leaned her head back against the booth and closed her eyes.

"You had options," he continued. He knew she couldn't see those options at the time.

"Yeah, like what?" She straightened in her seat.

"You could've talked to a counselor. You were on a scholarship. They could have helped you find financing so you could keep your apartment."

"It's too late," she moaned.

"No, it's not. Call them. You could get back in next semester," he urged. If only she would listen to him now.

"I asked for an incomplete in all my classes before the funeral. I couldn't concentrate enough to study for the finals."

"I know." María did need time to grieve. She had no one to confide in at the time, either. Her mother had just given up the fight with pneumonia. She longed to be with her husband, but he couldn't explain that to María.

∼

María closed her eyes and inhaled deeply, letting her breath out slowly through her mouth.

Her mother had been a nurse and ever since she was a little girl, she had wanted to be one, too, but her circumstances had changed with her mother's recent death. The money had simply run out.

She opened her eyes. Living on the streets had become dangerous. There were too many things going on lately that scared her, and tonight was the worst.

"Promise me you'll call them," Mike said softly, his brows raised with hopeful anticipation.

She looked at him, at those piercing brown eyes. How could she say no? "I promise." She looked down at her hands, folded on the table. Her initial thoughts of Mike came to mind. "You, uh, didn't hear what I had been thinking earlier, did you?"

"Of course I did." He set his coffee down and pinned her with an intense look, then he winked.

She tensed her jaws and felt her cheeks grow hot.

He smiled at her. There was something so sexy about the way he looked at her, it threw her off guard. No one had ever looked at her that way.

You are a very beautiful young woman. She heard his voice in her head, an audible sound.

"Yeah, right," she mumbled. "A woman who sleeps in dumpsters and wears over-sized men's suits?"

He crossed his arms over his chest. *You could change all that, you know.* His voice was audible again, but only in her mind.

"Why haven't you shown yourself to me before?"

"It wasn't necessary until now," Mike said.

She thought of all the times she had felt lonely and could have used a friend. She lowered her head and sipped her coffee. "So, after tonight, do you disappear again...forever?" The thought saddened her. She glanced up into his eyes.

"If you want me to, I will."

"No! I...mean, I like your company. Don't go." She lowered her eyes once more.

"I'll always be here, whether you see me or not," he said.

"Yes, but I wouldn't be able to talk to you," she said, gazing into his dark brown eyes.

"Of course you can talk to me," he said, touching her forearm.

The warmth from his hand ran throughout her body instantaneously, like someone turned the heat up with the flick of a wrist.

"I wouldn't be able to hear you, though, would I?"

"If you pay attention, you can hear me when I speak to your mind."

"What about Joe Blue? I need to tell someone about what happened, don't I?" she whispered.

"Yes, but it can wait until later this morning. The police will find him and make a report. You'll be able to fill in the missing pieces for them later."

"Were you an angel when you were a...cop?" She sipped her coffee but didn't move the arm he was touching. She drew comfort from his nearness.

Mike glanced away momentarily, then back at her. "No. I...was...I don't remember being a cop. Being your Guardian Angel is all I know."

"Will that change now?" Her heart rate increased slightly at the thought of losing his company.

"No. I will always be your Guardian Angel." He gave her arm a squeeze.

"Yeah, but now I'll have to find a bigger dumpster to sleep in."

He yanked her hat from her head, then mussed her hair.

"Hey? What did you do that for?" she said, reaching for the hat he held above her head.

"I've always wanted to do that," he said. Their gazes locked. "You have the prettiest hair I've ever seen."

She lowered her eyes then looked back into his. "Thank you." The few moments of teasing endeared him to her. Her father had teased her when she was growing up and she missed it.

He set her hat down and caught her hands in his, running the pads of his thumbs against her palms. "You are a beautiful young woman. Quit hiding behind these...ugly clothes."

"You know why I do it," she whispered, lowering her eyes once more. Another month of working and she would be able to pay her back rent. Then Mr. Turner would give her the contents of the apartment, but she would still be homeless, unless she could come up with another month's rent.

"I know." Mike slowly pulled his hands away but held her sad gaze.

"Tell me, Mike, what you remember...about your past?" she asked, changing the subject.

"Like I said before, all I remember is being your Guardian Angel. I didn't know that I had a past." He looked up to heaven, then back at her. "But the taste of the coffee and food are familiar to me, as if I had them before."

~

When Mike had caressed her hands, warmth emanated from her flesh and burned into him, making another memory he wouldn't forget. The feel of her silky hair beneath his fingers, and her soft, smooth skin brought on that strange sensation he had experienced earlier. It was a pleasing sensation that alerted his body in a way that was familiar yet new. And he didn't want the sensations to stop. In fact, he wanted to touch more of her flesh—

"Were you...married?" Her question interrupted his thoughts.

"I...don't remember," he said, searching his mind for anything that could answer that question. A question he never would have entertained had he remained a spirit being.

She looked at him differently now, with an expectancy he had never seen before. His heart rate increased.

Why was he having these flashes of memories while in the flesh and why these new feelings?

"Here's your check," Susan said, turning the paper upside down in front of him.

María took the receipt and looked at it, then pulled her change purse out of her coat pocket. Withdrawing enough funds to cover the two meals plus a tip, she left the money on the table.

"I'll be right back," she said, getting up. She headed for the restroom.

Mike couldn't let her out of his sight, so he turned back into a spirit being.

María returned to the dining room, but Mike was nowhere in sight. Some Guardian Angel he turned out to be.

"Hmmm." He helped her spend her money and then took off. She'd been on a couple of dates that ended that way. Why did she always fall for guys like that? She didn't even see it coming. She stepped out the door and looked up and down the deserted street. The bus wouldn't be running for another hour.

The Greasy Spoon was a couple miles from there. The walk would do her good with all she had to think about.

Having breakfast with an angel was a new experience for her, especially one as good looking as Mike. She shoved her hands in her pockets as a cool, crisp breeze stirred the air. She thought about the cute dimple on Mike's face.

She headed downtown on Ninth Avenue. How many other people had seen their Guardian Angel, she wondered. There was something about him that fascinated her. More questions formed in her head as she walked. She didn't get to ask why he dressed the way he did, or how he transported them across town. Had she imagined the past hour?